E
Mon   Moncure, Jane Belk
        My "g" sound box

ENCYCLOPAEDIA BRITANNICA
EDUCATIONAL CORPORATION
310 S. Michigan Avenue • Chicago, Illinois 60604
85358

My

Sound Box

g

by Jane Belk Moncure
illustrated by Linda Sommers

THE CHILD'S WORLD

MANKATO, MN 56001

Library of Congress Cataloging in Publication Data

Moncure, Jane Belk.
  My g sound box.

  (Sound box books)
  SUMMARY: A little girl fills her sound box with
many words that begin with the letter "g".
  [1. Alphabet] I. Sommers, Linda. II. Title.
III. Series.
PZ7.M739Myg   [E]   78-22037
ISBN 0-89565-053-3 -1991 Edition

My "g" Sound Box

(This book uses only the hard "g" sound in the story line. Blends are included. Words beginning with the soft "g" sound are included at the end of the book.)

Little  g had a box.

"I will find things that begin with my 'g' sound," she said.

"I will put them into my sound  box."

Little g opened the gate

and went into the garden.

Little g found

goats

in the garden.

Did she put the goats into her box?

She did.

Then Little g found grass,

lots and lots of green grass.

She put the green grass into the box with the goats.

But the goats ate it all up!

Little g found grapes,

lots and lots of grapes.

She put the grapes into the box.

But the goats ate up all the grapes too!

What could Little  g do?

She found a gorilla in the garden.

She put the gorilla into the box with the goats.

Did the goats eat the gorilla? No!

The goats grinned.

And so the gorilla grinned.

Little g found a guitar.

She played the guitar.

The gorilla danced.

Then the goats danced with the gorilla.

Everyone giggled!

Little  g found some glasses.

She put glasses on the goats.

Then she found goggles.

She put goggles on the gorilla.

Just then a
goose and gander walked by.

"What funny goats! What a funny gorilla!"
said the goose and gander.

Little 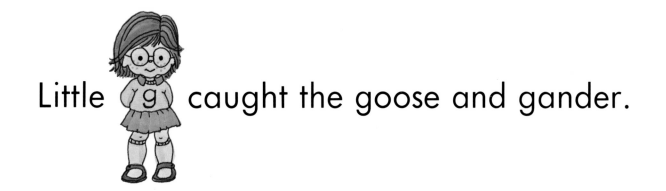 caught the goose and gander.

"You belong in my sound box," she said.

The goose got into the box all by herself.
"I will give you a gift," she said.

Then the goose laid an egg made of gold.
All of it was gold!

"What a great gift!" said Little ⓖ.

Little  looked around her garden.

grapes

gander

guitar

egg of gold

goose

"And what a great group of 'g's," she said.

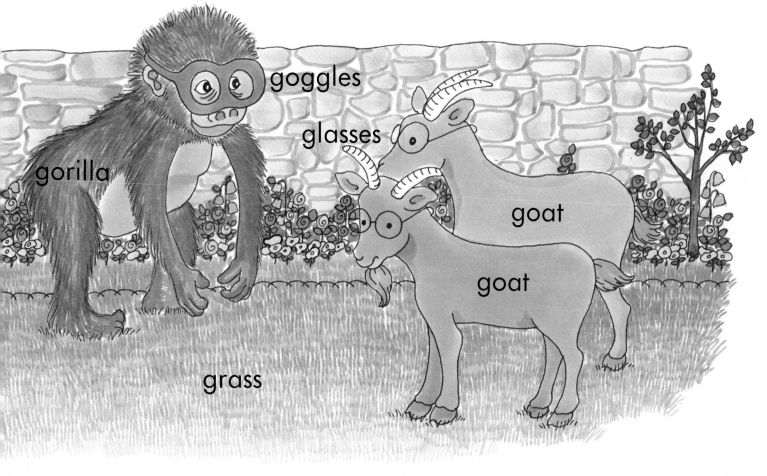

gorilla

goggles

glasses

goat

goat

grass

Can you read these words with Little ?

gum

goldfish

glass

gull

gumdrop

globe

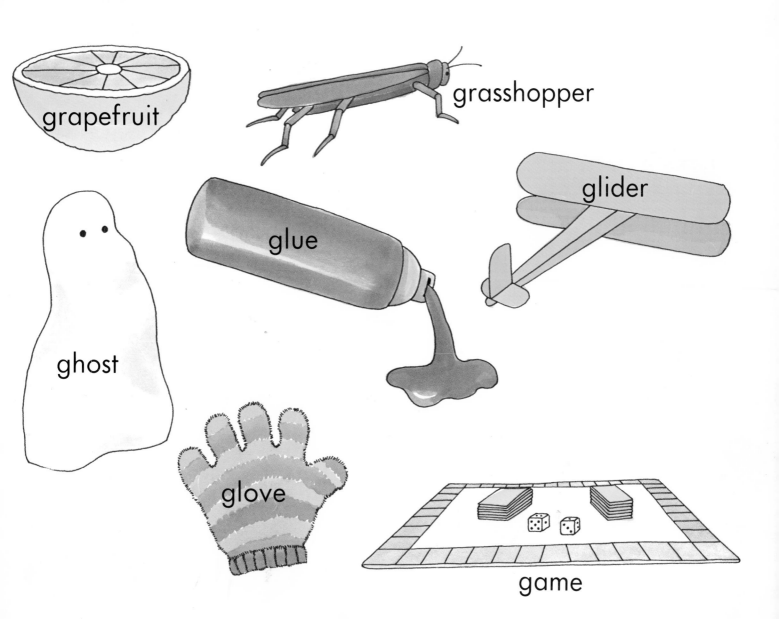

grapefruit

grasshopper

glider

glue

ghost

glove

game

In this sound-box story, Little  has her own special hard sound.

Little g has another sound too. It is soft, like the sound of the letter ''j''.

Can you read these words? Listen for the soft sound.

geranium

gingerbread

giraffe

gerbil

gypsy

About the Author

Jane Belk Moncure, author of many books and stories for young children, is a graduate of Virginia Commonwealth University and Columbia University. She has taught nursery, kindergarten and primary children in Europe and America. Mrs. Moncure has taught early childhood education while serving on the faculties of Virginia Commonwealth University and the University of Richmond. She was the first president of the Virginia Association for Early Childhood Education and has been recognized widely for her services to young children. She is married to Dr. James A. Moncure, Vice President of Elon College, and currently teaches in Burlington, North Carolina.